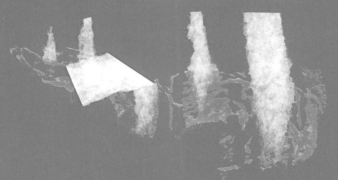

Originally published in the United States in 1993 by Houghton Mifflin Company. First published in Great Britain in 1995 by Andersen Press
Ltd., 20 Vauxhall Bridge Road, London SW1V 2SA. Published in Australia by Random House Australia Pty., 20 Alfred Street, Milsons Point,
Sydney, NSW 2061. All rights reserved. Colour separated in Switzerland by Photolitho AG, Offsetreproduktionen, Gossau, Zürich. Printed
and bound in Italy by Grafiche AZ, Verona.

10   9   8   7   6   5   4   3   2   1

British Library Cataloguing in Publication Data available.

ISBN 0 86264 498 4

This book has been printed on acid-free paper

The Sweetest Fig

CHRIS VAN ALLSBURG

Andersen Press • London

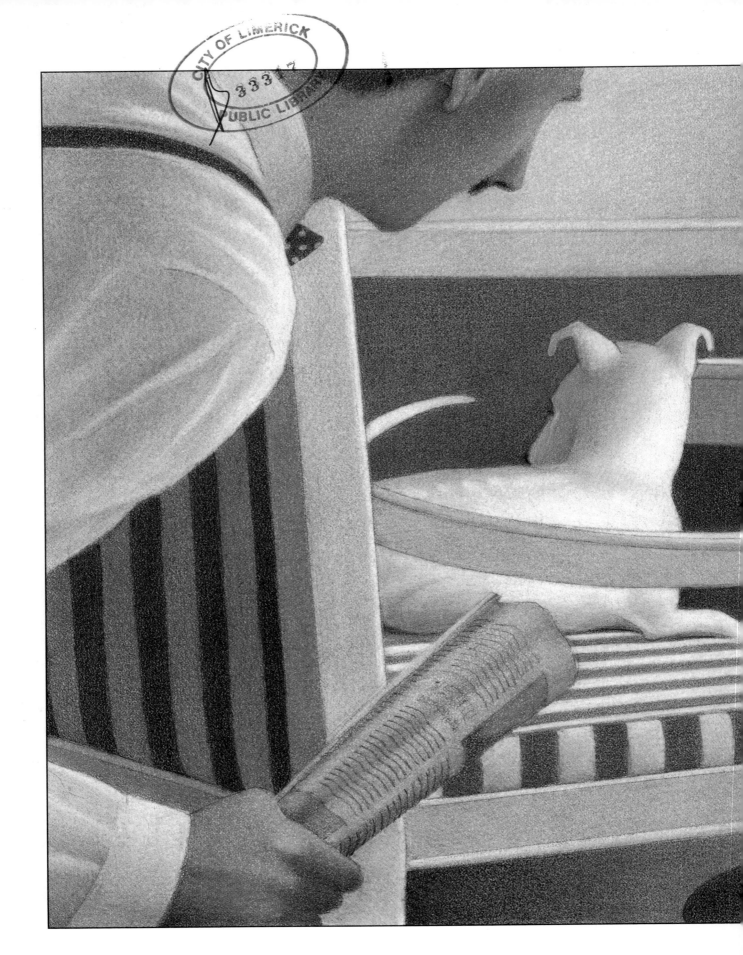

Monsieur Bibot, the dentist, was a very fussy man. He kept his small apartment as neat and clean as his office. If his dog, Marcel, jumped on the furniture, Bibot was sure to teach him a lesson. Except on Bastille Day, the poor animal was not even allowed to bark.

One morning, Bibot met an old woman waiting at his office door. She had a toothache and begged the dentist to help.

"But you have no appointment," he told her.

The woman moaned. Bibot looked at his watch. Perhaps there was time to make a few extra francs. He took her inside and looked in her mouth. "This tooth must come out," he said with a smile.

When he was done, the dentist said, "I will give you some pills to kill the pain."

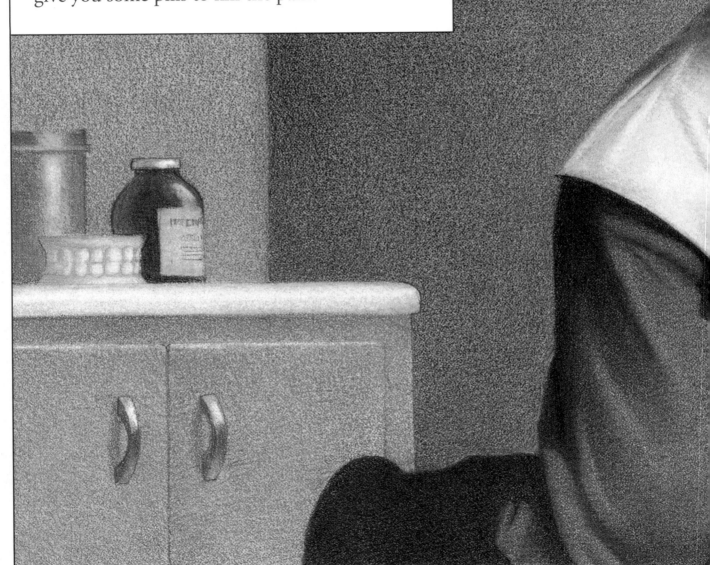

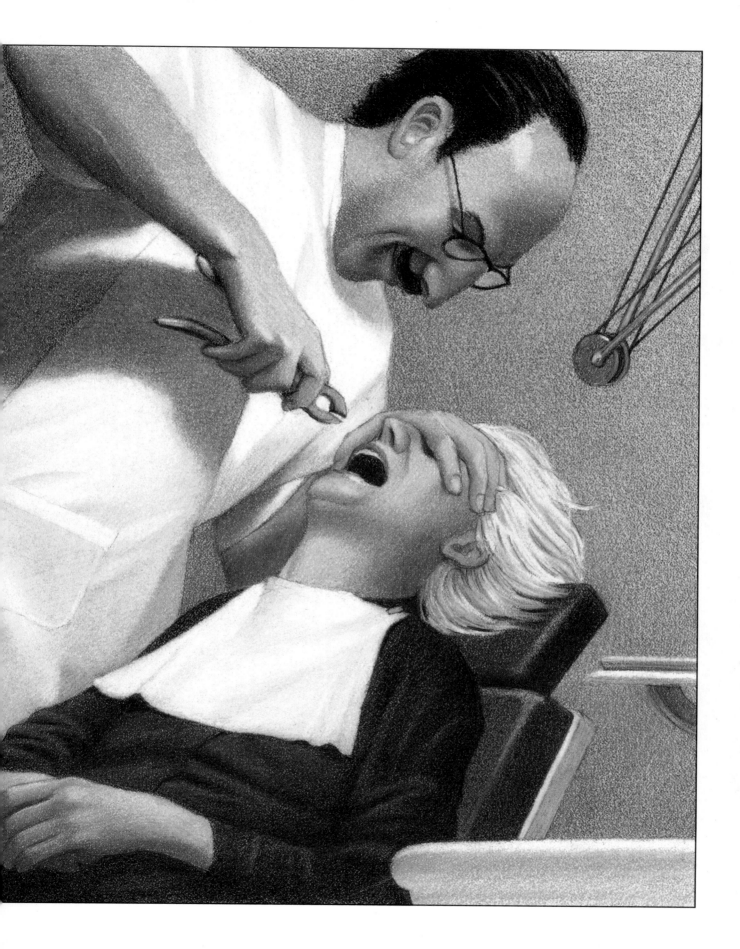

The old woman was very grateful. "I can't pay you in money, but I have something much better." She took two figs from her pocket and handed them to Bibot.

"Figs!?" he said angrily.

"These figs are very special," the woman whispered. "They can make your dreams come true." She winked at him and put her finger to her lips.

It was clear to Bibot that the woman was crazy. He set the figs down and took her by the arm. When she reminded him about the pills, he said, "I'm sorry, only for paying customers," and shoved her out the door.

That evening, Bibot took his little dog to the park. Poor Marcel loved to sniff the tree trunks and bushes, but whenever he stopped, Bibot would pull sharply on the lead.

Just before going to bed, the dentist had a small snack. He sat at his dining room table and ate one of the figs the old woman had given him. It was delicious. Possibly the finest, sweetest fig he'd ever had.

In the morning, Bibot dragged Marcel down the stairs for his morning walk. The steep steps were hard for the short-legged dog, but Bibot wouldn't think of carrying his pet. He hated to get Marcel's white hairs on his beautiful blue suit.

As he walked along the crowded pavement, Bibot could not help noticing people looking at him. "They are admiring my suit," he thought. But when Bibot saw his reflection in the window of a café, he stopped in horror. He was dressed only in his underwear.

The dentist turned and ran into an alley. "Sacré bleu," he thought. "What has happened to my clothes?" Then he remembered the dream he'd had last night. In his dream, he'd stood in front of that very café, dressed in his underwear.

Something else had happened in his dream, and Bibot struggled to recall it. Marcel, looking out from the shadows of the alley, began to bark. The dentist looked up and saw the rest of his dream come true.

No one noticed Bibot as he ran home
in his underwear. All the eyes of Paris
were fixed on the Eiffel Tower, which
slowly drooped over as if it were made of
soft rubber.

Bibot understood now that the old
woman with the figs had told him the
truth. He would not waste the second fig.

Over the next few weeks, as reconstruction of the Eiffel Tower began, the dentist read dozens of books on hypnotism. Each night before he went to sleep, he gazed into a mirror and whispered over and over, "Bibot is the richest man on earth, Bibot is the richest man on earth."

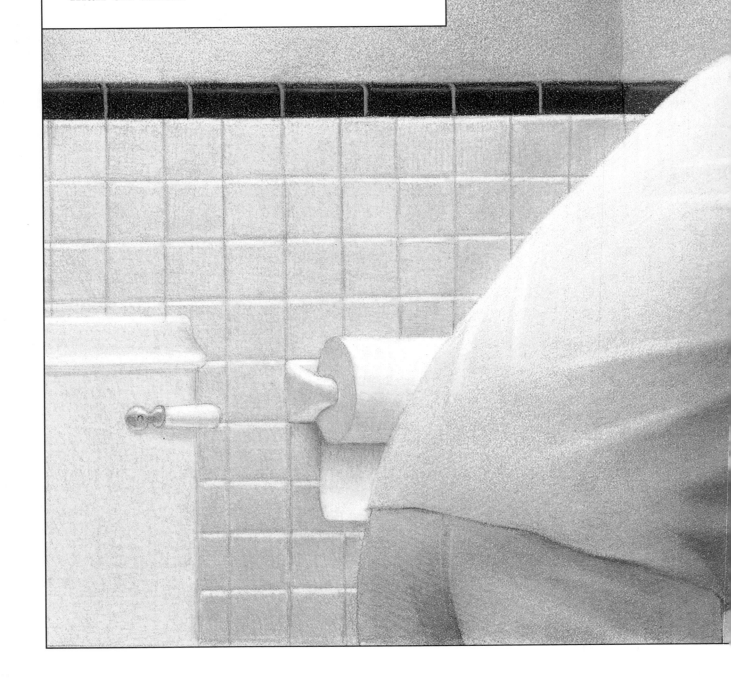

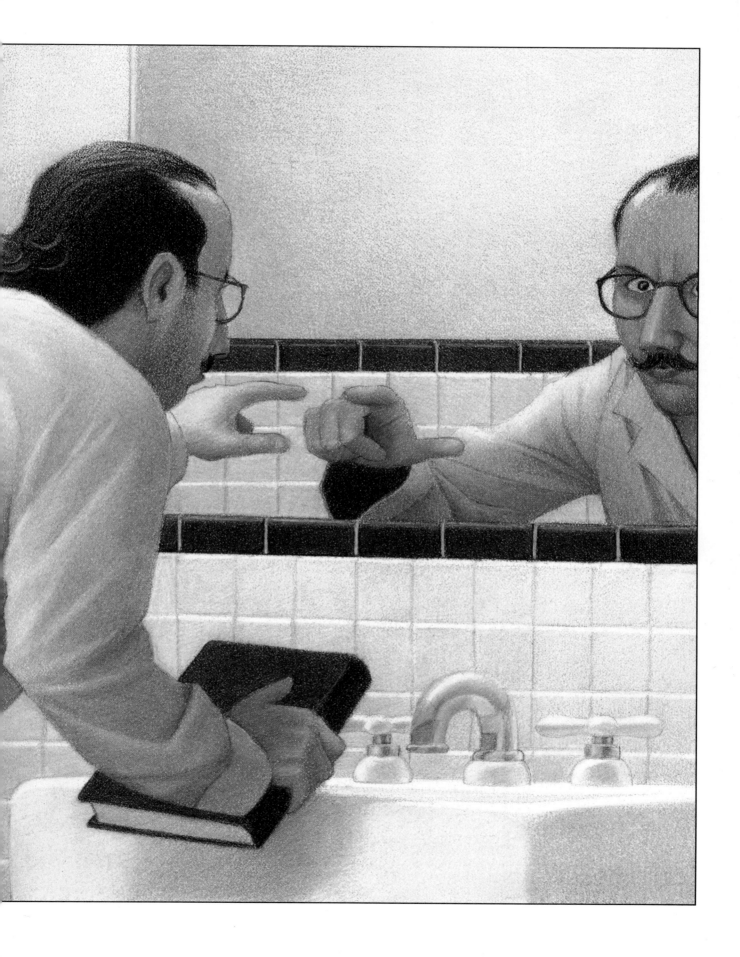

Soon, in his dreams, that's exactly what he was. As he slept, the dentist saw himself steering his speedboat, flying his aeroplane, and living in luxury on the Riviera. Night after night it was the same.

One evening, Bibot took the second fig from his cupboard. It would not last forever. "Tonight," he thought, "is the night." He put the ripe fruit on a dish and set it on his table. Tomorrow he would wake up the richest man in the world. He looked down at Marcel and smiled. The little dog would not be coming along. In his dreams Bibot had Great Danes.

As the dentist reached into his cupboard to take out some cheese, he heard the crash of breaking china. He turned to see Marcel standing on a chair with his front paws on the table, chewing the last of the fig.

Bibot was furious! He chased the dog around the apartment. When Marcel ran beneath the bed Bibot yelled at him, "Tomorrow, I'll teach you a lesson you'll never forget!" Then the dentist, angry and heartbroken, went to sleep.

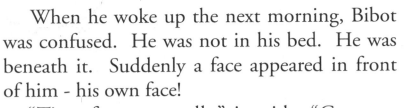

When he woke up the next morning, Bibot was confused. He was not in his bed. He was beneath it. Suddenly a face appeared in front of him - his own face!

"Time for your walk," it said. "Come to Marcel." A hand reached down and grabbed him. Bibot tried to yell, but all he could do was bark.